Brought to you by

This book belongs to

_____.

My birthday is on

_____.

Toys "R" us

Designed by Georgia Rucker
Published by Downtown Bookworks Inc.
265 Canal Street, New York, NY 10013

PRINTED IN THE U.S.A., FEBRUARY 2016

THE LEGEND OF GEOFFREY

WRITTEN BY Piro

ILLUSTRATED BY Dubravka Kolanovic

downtown bookworks

Geoffrey was a very busy giraffe. There were
tasty leaves to munch, colorful friends to meet,
and super-fun games to play all day long.

Every night, Geoffrey was enchanted by
a zillion dazzling stars in the sky.

One warm night, Geoffrey decided he wanted
to touch a star. He climbed the highest hill he could
find and stretched until the tip of his nose touched
the lowest star.

And when it did, the whole night sky came to life.
Geoffrey watched the stars twinkle until he could not
keep his eyes open any longer.

Under these stars, surrounded by the things he
loved, Geoffrey was home.

The next morning when he woke up, Geoffrey felt different inside—a little more special than usual. And he *looked* different too: his brown spots had turned into sparkling stars! If that wasn't strange enough, there was also a little monkey trying hard to get his attention.

"I'm Maya," announced the friendly monkey. "Cool stars! Do you want to play?" she asked.

Of course Geoffrey wanted to play! He watched Maya swing from branch to branch, and then he gave it a try.

But giraffes were not meant to swing from tree branches.

So he made up a different game. Geoffrey was pretty good at this one. He and Maya were having so much fun they didn't even notice that . . .

. . . a pride of lions had circled them.

"Hello, Dessert," said the largest lion, licking his chops.

"A-a-actually, my name is Geoffrey," stammered the giraffe. "Would you like some nice, sweet a-a-apricots?" Geoffrey offered up a hoof-ful, shaking with fear.

The lion was about to take a bite out of Geoffrey when he noticed the giraffe's coat. "Stars!" he exclaimed. "This is no ordinary giraffe."

The lion bowed down to Geoffrey as he explained, "There is a famous legend that, one day, an animal covered in stars will appear and bring awesome fun to the world." The lions all nodded. Geoffrey *was* covered in stars. But could it be true?

"I'm no legend. I'm just Geoffrey," he told them.

The lion smirked, "Well, if you're not the legend, then you're lunch." Geoffrey quickly agreed that he was *absolutely, positively* the star-covered wonder from the legend.

The lion told him, kindly, "You have the gift of awesomeness. You must follow the stars to find your destiny."

But before he followed the stars, Geoffrey wanted to find out what, exactly, was so awesome about him.

He challenged Charlie the Cheetah to a race.

He lost.
He did not have awesome running powers.

He challenged Finnegan the Flamingo to a standing-on-one-leg contest.

He lost again.
He did not have special balancing powers.

He thought maybe, just maybe, he could fly.

Nope. No flying powers.

"Maybe you just need to follow the stars and figure out your awesomeness along the way," suggested Maya.

"The only stars I can see are over there." Geoffrey pointed out in the distance.

Geoffrey and Maya made their way across the dry golden grass. And wherever they went, the grass turned lush and green as if by magic. As they got closer, they realized the stars were actually twinkling lights strung on a big, beautiful ship.
"This looks like the next step on your journey," said Maya, as the two friends hugged goodbye.

Geoffrey boarded the ship, excited to see where the stars would lead him.

After many days and nights
sailing across the sea, the ship
docked in New York City.

Geoffrey got a bite to eat and took a good look around at the buildings and strange little creatures.

He started to feel lost and far from home. He thought about Maya and the lions who told him about the legend—the legend that said he should follow the stars.

But which stars?!

Should he
follow the stars
on Broadway?

No, these were
probably not the
right stars.

That gigantic spinning star
seemed to be calling his name!

But it just
made him dizzy.

Maybe he needed to
get even closer to the
night sky to find his way?

But not *that* close.

THE CYCLONE

Toys ЯUs

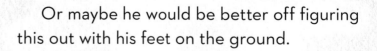

Or maybe he would be better off figuring
this out with his feet on the ground.

17

He was trying to
decide which way he
should go when . . .

. . . he spied a monkey on the
street who reminded him of Maya.
Geoffrey lifted the worn little
stuffed animal.

As he did, the monkey magically
came to life!

"Who are you?" demanded the
scrappy stuffed animal. "Where is Lulu?"

"Umm . . . that way?" Geoffrey
pointed at the pedicab up ahead, where
they could just see the red pom-pom on
a little girl's pink hat.

He and the monkey jumped in a taxi and pointed the way.

But there were so many cars that soon they couldn't see the red pom-pom or any sign of Lulu at all, so they hopped out . . .

ILEE 1449

... and sat down on the sidewalk.

"Thank you," said the monkey. "My name is Patches, by the way."

"I'm Geoffrey," he replied, taking the monkey's paw in his hoof.

"How did you do that magic thing?" Patches wanted to know.

"Magic thing?" asked Geoffrey.

"You know, I could never talk or do anything else . . . until you picked me up."

"Seriously?"

"If you don't believe me, let's see if your magic works on them," Patches suggested, pointing at the store window filled with stuffed animals.

So Geoffrey ducked through a big glass door into the
most amazing place he had ever seen. "It's Toys"R"Us,
the world's greatest toy store," whispered Patches. There
were toy trucks and trains, robots and rockets, tents
and playhouses. And best of all, there were zebras and
elephants and all of the other animals he grew up with.

Patches said, "OK, Geoffrey—
now try your magic!"

Geoffrey's eyes lit up. His stars
began to shimmer as he ran through
the store and, with the slightest tap of
a hoof, brought the toys to life.

A very serious chess piece, the
Queen, took it all in—the scooters
scooting, toy trains tooting, and
superheroes soaring overhead.
"It's our birthday!" she announced
to Geoffrey.

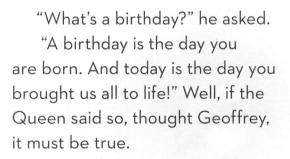

"What's a birthday?" he asked.
"A birthday is the day you
are born. And today is the day you
brought us all to life!" Well, if the
Queen said so, thought Geoffrey,
it must be true.

That night, the toys had the most
awesome birthday party ever.

Early the next day, a parade of excited little children began
to file into Toys"R"Us.

"Happy birthday!" said one sweet grandma to her young
grandson. "Now let's see what awesome toy we can find
for you!"

When Geoffrey heard "happy birthday," his velvety ears
perked up. A real-life birthday! Geoffrey began to stack some
wooden blocks.

The little boy ran to the tower of colorful blocks, and his
grandmother smiled.

"Happy birthday!" said a man in paint-splattered pants to his daughter. "Let's find a great present for you!"

Geoffrey went to work again. "Excuse me," he said to the little girl. "Every artist needs an easel!" Her eyes lit up.

"Thank you!" whispered the easel to Geoffrey.

"Thanks, Geoffrey!" said the colorful blocks.

Things were going so well that Geoffrey was surprised to see Patches looking a little sad.

Geoffrey tried to give his friend a hug. But when your neck is six feet long, a hug can get a little messy.

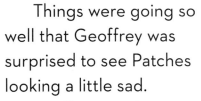

Patches and Geoffrey tried
to clean up, but that only made
things worse.

So they decided
it was best to scoot
out of the way.

Patches smiled at Geoffrey. "You're a really good friend," he said, "but I miss being home with Lulu."

A shiny red fire truck piped in, "I would love to find a home."

"We would all love to find homes and kids to be friends with," added a funny little robot.

"Well, then I will find a home for each of you," Geoffrey promised. His stars began to glow, and the toys hummed with excitement.

One by one, Geoffrey
went about finding the
perfect child to take home
each of his new friends.

Geoffrey and Patches looked around at all of the happy children heading out of the store with their new toys when, suddenly, they spotted Lulu!

They hopped on a scooter and raced over to Lulu just in time. "I think this monkey will be perfect for you," Geoffrey told her.

"Patches! I thought I would never see you again!" Lulu squealed. She hugged her long-lost friend and looked up at Geoffrey. "Thank you for finding him."

Looking out at the stars in the city sky, Geoffrey was happy. He knew now that his destiny was to find the perfect toys for children and the perfect homes for toys.

Under these stars, surrounded by the friends he loved, Geoffrey was finally home again.